TAV

D0345828

**This Orchard
book belongs to**

_____

_____

_____

ORCHARD BOOKS

96 Leonard Street, London, EC2A 4XD

Orchard Books Australia

32/45-51 Huntley Street, Alexandria, NSW 2015

ISBN 1 84362 790 6

First published in Great Britain in 1997

First published in paperback in 1998

This edition published in 2005

Text and illustrations © Adrian Reynolds 1997

The right of Adrian Reynolds to be identified as the author and illustrator

of this work has been asserted by him in accordance

with the Copyright, Designs and Patents Act, 1998.

A CIP catalogue record for this book is available from the British Library.

Printed in Hong Kong, China

1 3 5 7 9 10 8 6 4 2

GIFT

Pete and Polo

Hide-and-Seek

Adrian Reynolds

ORCHARD BOOKS

For my Mum and Dad

Every day, when breakfast is over,
Pete and Polo set off on an adventure together.

They climb the highest mountains together...

they hide in the deepest darkest caves together...

they explore the most dangerous tiger-infested
jungles together…

and they battle with huge scary monsters.

One afternoon, after escaping from a dangerous monster, Pete and Polo met Mum at the door.

"Oh, Pete," she said. "Just look at the state of Polo. You really should take better care of him."

"I am a bit dirty," said Polo. Pete had to agree.

The next morning Polo
was nowhere to be seen.
"That's strange," said Pete.
"Polo always waits for me.
Perhaps he's playing hide-and-seek."
Pete went searching for him.

Polo wasn't hiding in the deep dark cave...

he wasn't climbing up the mountain…

Pete searched through the dangerous jungle
but Polo wasn't there either.

Pete was afraid that Polo had been gobbled up
by the huge scary monster.

Pete began to search the whole house.
He looked under the stairs…

he looked on top of shelves...

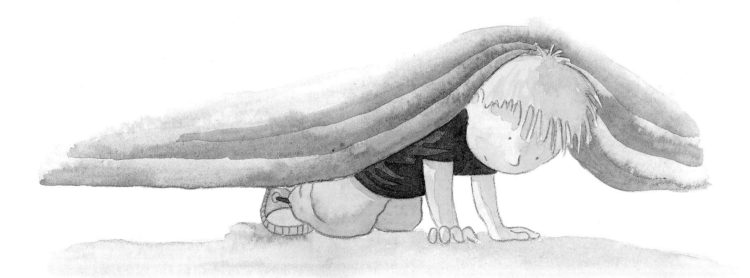

he looked under the beds...

he looked behind the curtains...

and he even looked in the rubbish bin...

but Polo was nowhere to be found.

By this time Pete was feeling very
sad and lonely and a little bit sniffy.

Suddenly Mum appeared, and there
was Polo! He looked all clean and white.
"Look, Pete," he said. "I'm not
dirty any more. I've been having
an adventure all by myself.
I've been swimming in
deep bubbly seas."

Pete wanted to give Polo
a great big hug.

"Wait," cried Polo. "Look at
the state you're in. You can't
hug me until you're clean.
It's your turn to go swimming."

And Pete had to agree.

Pete and Polo both agreed that
swimming in deep bubbly seas
was quite an adventure too.

D0347269